Sha'Tanya

UNDONE

Sha'Tanya
UNDONE

MARIO HERBERT

CONTENTS

Introduction

This is the story of Sha'Tanya Carter, a snarky, popular teenage girl with no lack of confidence, and no reservations about pointing out when others are in error.

Like any other teenager, she's still learning the lessons of life through ill-fated relationships, bitter rivalries and questionable decisions.

Intriguing adventures and painful lessons were already chronicled in *Sha'Tanya Unleashed*, but Sha'Tanya still has a lot of lessons to learn.

The stories you are about to read span two years, coincide with events seen in *Adrian at Large* and *Adrian at Last*, and reference themes explored in *Adrian at Loggerheads*.

These chronicles are not required reading, however, and have no impact on the life altering events which lie ahead, so turn the page and let the adventures begin!

DETOUR

The wind howled like a pack of wolves in a chorus of unison as rain shot down in unruly torrents. Sha'Tanya peeped from under her blanket, through the window of her lamplit room, where she could barely see the silhouette of bending trees through the torrents of rain blowing wildly in heavy gusts. Suddenly, the room was illuminated with a blindingly bright flash, followed by a thunderous crash that shook the house. The room was instantly thrown into darkness as the light from the lamp and the nearby streetlight perished.

Sha'Tanya sat up in her bed, startled by the flash, the crash and the sudden darkness. Suddenly, the wind seemed to increase its speed, and the rain intensified its attack. Sha'Tanya's heart went into overdrive; the howling wind and crashing thunder were scary on their own, but the total blackness which now surrounded her, seemed to increase the eeriness of those sounds tenfold.

Suddenly, Sha'Tanya heard the familiar creaking

sound of her bedroom door opening, and a figure appeared, carrying a large, lit candle.

"I know my daughter ain't gonna admit to being scared," said the partially lit figure, in a feminine voice, "so I'm bringing a candle for her."

"Scared?" cried Sha'Tanya, in a brave tone, careful not to betray her throbbing heart. "Error! I'm a big girl in third form."

At that moment, there was a dreadful sound. A bright flash of lightning provided enough illumination for Sha'Tanya to see the roof from the house next-door, being ripped off by the wind. The crashing thunder that followed was accompanied by the crashing sound of galvanised roofing sheets hitting unknown objects after being blown off the house. Sha'Tanya's heart beat even faster as the combined, crashing sounds sent a chill through her body. She felt some relief as she felt her mother's arm around her shoulder, but she refused to show any outward signs of fear.

Her calm veneer was soon tested, as a new, terrifying sound was introduced; Sha'Tanya could hear the galvanised sheets on her own roof, flapping in the wind. Immediately, the sight of her neighbour's roof being lifted off the house flashed before her. Sha'Tanya could pretend no longer, and she promptly embraced her mother tightly. The sound steadily intensified; it sounded like the nails were being pulled out of the rafters. Sha'Tanya started to tremble, fearful of what could happen. Her entire life in that house flashed before her; she couldn't imagine how her life would change if her house were to be compromised. Then, her mother uttered a single sentence which completely broke her.

"Go, pack a bag of essentials, quickly," said her mother, with urgency in her voice, "we have to get out of here."

Sha'Tanya broke down in tears as she started to gather her essentials by candlelight, as her mother left the room to do the same. All the while, as she packed, the sounds intensified, chilling her to her core as her heart pounded at a new, record-breaking speed. As she packed her hair gel and zipped her backpack, she was startled by a sound more terrifying than anything she had heard that night; the roof was ripped off her house and a gust of wind extinguished the candle before she felt herself being drenched by torrents of rain.

"Grab the bag and come," came her mother's loud voice, through the blackness, "we gotta make a run for the neighbour."

As soon as Sha'Tanya ran out of the room, her mother grabbed her hand and the pair ran out of the house and started for the nearest house which was still intact. As they valiantly fought their way through the gusty winds, heavy rain and thick blackness, afforded brief moments of visibility by flashes of lightning, Sha'Tanya could hear a terrible crash behind her as the wooden portion of her house was demolished by the raging hurricane. That crash didn't only represent the end of her house, but the end of life as she had known it.

One week later, the island of Barbados was back to partial normalcy; while there were still some blocked roads and fallen infrastructure, power had been largely restored, most businesses had reopened and schools were about to resume classes.

Life for Sha'Tanya, however, was far from normal. She had moved into her grandmother's unit in a government-run apartment block. There, she shared the smallest of three bedrooms with her mother. They slept together on a twin-sized bed—the only size bed that could fit in the cramped room. There was a single louver-style window at the foot of the bed, and two small chests of drawers on the right side of the bed, adjacent to the door. Being cramped in this small room with her mother represented a major loss of independence for Sha'Tanya. Her bedroom, however, wasn't the only discomforting aspect of her new residence.

Downstairs, the kitchen and dining area was a single room and the living room and bathroom were smaller than those at Sha'Tanya's former residence. Upstairs, were the bedrooms, which were inundated by a bevy of other family members who had moved into the house in the aftermath of the hurricane. The bedroom next to Sha'Tanya's housed three cousins, while two aunts shared the largest room with her grandmother.

Having eight people in a cramped house was a big change for Sha'Tanya, who was accustomed to living with her mother alone. Not only were there more people in her space, but there was a big clash of different personalities and habits. Different people hung their underwear all over the bathroom, there was always some measure of noise in the house, and her grandmother was prone to senile moments.

DETOUR

Sha'Tanya was ashamed of her new home, house-mates and neighbourhood, which consisted of many riffraff elements. She would have preferred to live with her father but his house was severely damaged as well, putting him in a similar position. The only saving grace was that barring her best friend, Laurel, none of her school friends knew her new address, nor her living conditions. As she prepared to resume her classes, she was intent on keeping it that way.

On her first day back at school, there was no indication that anything was different. Her hair glistened as the usual flood of hair gel placed it in suspended animation on her head. Not even the persistent showers of that day could dampen her perky, snarky attitude. Deep down inside, however, she was deeply damaged by the trauma of losing her house, and deeply ashamed of her current living conditions.

Throughout the day, the topic of conversation among students was the hurricane and its effects. Sha'Tanya was very measured in what information she surrendered. By the end of the school day, her friends, classmates and acquaintances knew that she had lost her house, and moved to her grandmother's house, but they didn't know the finer details; she gave them a generalised location, but didn't specify whether she lived in the upscale or downscale region.

That afternoon, after the last bell had rung, Sha'Tanya was walking down a pathway under a long trellis, leading to the front parking lot and exit of the school. She was accompanied by a tall, thick, dark girl with corn rows—her best friend, Laurel. Also present, was a brown, medium height, medium build girl with her hair gelled into a bun—another friend of hers, Lystra.

"Don't look for me on the bus this evening," said Lystra, "my father's coming to pick me up."

"Lucky you," Laurel replied, with a sigh, "we gotta face this ugly weather."

"Speak of the devil," cried Lystra, pointing to a green sedan entering the parking lot. "You know, he's supposed to be meeting a friend in your area, 'Tan Tan'; we should be able to give you a ride."

Sha'Tanya paused, and pondered briefly, before accepting the offer.

"Cool," she replied, causing Laurel to give her an intent stare.

"Wait here," said Lystra, as she took off towards the car, "let me clear it with 'Pops' first."

"She just called her father 'Pops'?" Sha'Tanya cried, with a disgusted look on her face. "Error!"

"Reserve that 'error' for yourself," cried Laurel, arms akimbo, staring intently at Sha'Tanya, "I thought you' trying to keep your address a secret!"

"Be cool," replied Sha'Tanya, calmly, watching Lystra speak to her clear, spectacled father in the distance.

"Your head screwed on backwards?" asked Laurel, waving her arms franticly. "Lystra is a good friend, but you know she's an unplugged fridge—can't keep anything for long!"

"Firstly, my favourite bus is still off the road, getting repaired," started Sha'Tanya.

Normally, the girls would have been rushing for a seat in *Turbulence*, but it had collided with another bus at the beginning of the term.

"Secondly, with this weather, I ain't excited 'bout squeezing in a hot, windows-closed, rust-bucket bus, with a bunch of musty children," Sha'Tanya continued, with a snarky attitude, "and lastly, I can tell him to put me off somewhere nearby, and walk the rest of the way."

By this time, Lystra was beckoning Sha'Tanya to come to the car.

"You seem to have a plan," said Laurel, walking towards the driveway to exit the school as Sha'Tanya started for the car, "I gotta face these musty children by myself."

In short order, Sha'Tanya was exchanging pleasantries with Lystra's father and getting into the tan, upholstered back seat of the car. Lystra's father promptly proceeded to follow the driveway, along the east wall of the school, then along the playing field on the south side of the school, to the western back gate of the school; they were on their way.

The journey took longer than it would have normally taken, due to a number of unavoidable detours; some roads were still blocked and others were actively being cleared. As they drove, the conversation in the car, naturally, was about the hurricane. Sha'Tanya stayed out of it as much as possible—until Lystra's father, who worked at a distribution company, shared some information of interest to her.

"The hurricane may have passed but it's still impacting us," said Lystra's father, in a deep voice, "shipping is completely disrupted; deodorant, hair products and other cosmetic shipments are delayed for the moment."

"This man means to tell me that after losing my house, and having to squeeze into my grandmother's clown car of a house, I might soon be losing hair gel as well?" Sha'Tanya thought to herself, before verbalising her thoughts in a single word.

"Error!"

There was no time to discuss the possible hair gel apocalypse, however, as the car reached the outskirts of Sha'Tanya's general area.

"You can put me off anywhere around here," said Sha'Tanya, sharply changing the subject, "I can make my way from here."

"Unacceptable!" said the driver, firmly.

"You ain't understand," started Sha'Tanya, trying not to panic, "I gotta run an errand before going home."

"You will run your errand after I take you home," replied the parent, firmly, "the record will show that I returned you to your home in one piece."

"Cool," Sha'Tanya calmly replied, but inwardly, she was panicking. She couldn't allow the "unplugged fridge" to find out where she lived, but she could see that Lystra's father was firm in his resolve to take her directly to her house.

"How am I going to get out of this one?" she thought to herself, as the car moved through a middle-class residential area. "This man ain't stopping this car unless it's in front of my house."

Then, a thought hit her like a brick; nobody knew what her house looked like.

"That's where I'm going," she cried, leaning forward and pointing to a nice, two-story house with a guard wall.

"Woah," cried Lystra, "that is a nice house."

"Yeah," said Sha'Tanya, with a smile, as the car came to a stop, "I think Granny won the lottery or something."

Sha'Tanya exited the car promptly, feeling like a mouse released from a glue trap.

"Thank you, Mister …" started Sha'Tanya, as she stood in front of a small gate in the guard wall.

"You can call me Pops if you like," replied the driver, promptly.

"Error," she softly replied, with a disgusted look. "Thank you for the ride, sir."

"You're welcome … I'll move when you enter the property."

Sha'Tanya started to sweat a little; she had no idea how she would get herself out of this situation. To her relief, she glanced at the small gate, and realised that it was not locked. She immediately released the latch and walked through the gate. Realising the car had not yet moved, she proceeded to latch the gate again, then turned and walked across a well-kept lawn, towards the front porch of the house. As she walked, her heart was throbbing and her stomach was burning with anxiety. Finally, she reached the steps to the porch, and there was no indication of activity from Lystra's father. She proceeded to climb the steps, her heartrate climbing with every step. Finally, she crossed the porch and reached the front door, fearing her little game was over; she had no more moves left.

Suddenly, the sound of a horn pierced her ears, and she turned around to see the car moving off. She waved and then released a big sigh of relief. She walked over to the balcony of the porch, and gripped it for support as she allowed her heartrate and sweat glands to return to normal.

On this occasion, however, normalcy would be denied her. Before her heartrate could regulate, Sha'Tanya was startled by a low growl. She followed the sound with her eyes to see a black, midsized dog coming from the side of the house, around the porch. Far from returning to normal, her heart shot into overdrive, as the dog approached the steps, barking and snarling at her.

"Be cool, dog," she said, in a calm voice, hoping to somehow pacify the beast.

Suddenly, the dog darted up the stairs and into the porch. Fear and adrenaline overtook Sha'Tanya and she instinctively propelled herself over the balcony and took flight across the lawn. The backpack on her back was no obstacle, neither was her tight uniform; she shot across the lawn like a bullet.

As she ran towards the guard wall, she started to analyse her options. In addition to the small gate she had come through, there was a big gate, connected to a driveway which ran along the edge of the lawn to a garage at the side of the house. As she tried to figure out which gate would serve her best, she heard the dog a mere metre behind her and the plan changed; there was no time to fiddle with latches. Adrenaline took over like an autopilot, and propelled Sha'Tanya over the wall before the dog could catch her.

As she picked herself up off the sidewalk, in front of the property, her heart was pounding like a hammer on a construction site. She had escaped the property but the ordeal was far from over; the dog was trying to get over the small gate, and a middle-aged couple were pointing disapprovingly at her from across the street.

"She scaled that wall like a professional!" cried the short, clear female from across the road. "Jordan, you have to apprehend that thief!"

"Error!" cried a still winded Sha'Tanya, but before she could follow up that exclamation with an explanation, the clear man, of medium height and build, shot across the road towards her.

With a man running towards her and a dog trying to reach her, Sha'Tanya had no time to catch her breath, nor to regulate her heartrate. She shot off down the street like an athlete, with the man in hot pursuit.

Sha'Tanya wasn't well acquainted with the area but she had a good sense of direction, and could approximate the bearing needed to reach her home. She passed five houses before reaching the end of the street, then made a right turn onto another street of houses. Her pursuer kept a steady pace behind her, causing her to ponder her chances of escape.

"Lord, I need a miracle," she cried, as she ran.

Suddenly, she heard an expletive and looked back to see the man falling flat onto the sidewalk. She assumed he had tripped on something but she really didn't care how it had happened; it provided her a better chance of escape.

"Lord, I owe You one!" cried Sha'Tanya. "I promise I ain't going to insult Emelia Harris tomorrow!"

Sha'Tanya made a snap decision, crossing the roadway to make a left turn, instead of continuing along the street she was on. She soon discovered that this was a critical error; she had turned into a dead end—a short street with a garbage skip and a high wall at the end. She knew it was only a matter of time before her pursuer arrived, as she stood frozen, evaluating the wall before her. There was no time to waste; a decision needed to be made and action taken. She promptly climbed up onto the skip, and moved towards the wall, trying to balance on the edge of the skip.

As Sha'Tanya had postulated, it wasn't long before the man dashed into the cul-de-sac. He climbed up on the garbage skip, as Sha'Tanya had done a moment before, approached and scaled the wall, disappearing over the top in short order. It was at this point that Sha'Tanya emerged from the garbage skip.

"Error," she whispered, as she removed miscellaneous bits of filth from her person.

"Well, I guess it's a good thing I slipped and fell into the skip," she thought, as she exited the cul-de-sac and resumed her journey.

Her heartrate finally began to return to normal, though she remained slightly on edge for the remainder of her journey. By this time, the sky was sheeted with black clouds, and Sha'Tanya tried to maintain a brisk pace.

"I can't risk getting soaked by the rain," she thought, "that might wash out my hair gel."

Finally, her surroundings changed, heralding her arrival in lower-class territory; she wasn't far from home. It didn't take long for her to see government-run apartment blocks; she just had to navigate the blocks until she reached her own.

As she walked along a deteriorated road, reading the letter and number designations on the sides of the apartment blocks, a sharp voice pierced her ears.

"Hey, come here, sweet girl," came a rough, male voice.

Sha'Tanya looked around to see a boy who appeared to be in his late teens, rising from the step of an apartment. He was dark, with tall unkept hair. He wore a tattered, sleeveless shirt and a small, tight jeans which terminated about one hundred centimetres before his bare feet.

"I ain't got time for chitchat," said Sha'Tanya, continuing to walk at a brisk pace as the boy followed. "You see the sky, big man?"

"It's worth getting wet to spend some time with me, 'Sweetness'," replied the boy, still following, now with his arms outstretched.

"Hair got more knots than a climbing rope, shirt look like something from a yard sale, armpits look like the Amazon rain forest, and you want to spend time with me? cried Sha'Tanya, glancing back at the boy as she continued her brisk walk. "Error!"

"You actually insulting me on my own turf?" shouted the boy, angrily. "Let me see if you' still so mouthy when I get through with you!"

Sha'Tanya didn't know what that statement meant but after her recent experiences, she wasn't waiting around to find out. She shot off like a flare, with the barefooted boy in hot pursuit. At that moment it also started to rain, filling Sha'Tanya with despair. Her heart was pounding, her feet were tired and her countenance was darkened by the rain and dark clouds. As she approached the end of the block, she evaluated the junction ahead. To her despair, a car was speeding down the adjoining road, forcing her to come to a halt.

"Lord, I need another miracle," she whispered as she turned around to face her pursuer. He caught up to her just as the car zoomed past, and grabbed her by the throat.

Sha'Tanya started to panic as she struggled to no avail to release the boy's grip. She had prayed for a miracle but there wasn't a soul to be seen. The pouring rain mixed with her tears as her attacker leaned in as if to kiss her, and total despair overtook her.

Suddenly, her attacker recoiled, with a repulsed look on his face.

"Girl, you smell like you bathed in a landfill," cried the boy, releasing his grip on her throat, "what kind of riffraff girl …?"

Under normal circumstances, Sha'Tanya would have taken issue with someone calling her riffraff, but on this occasion, her fear was stronger than her attitude.

"I can't believe I waste' my charm on you," cried

the boy, turning away from Sha'Tanya.

"This boy's head put on backwards?" Sha'Tanya thought to herself. "He' got as much charm as a two-by-four."

"I ain't getting wet for a smelly, musty girl like you!" shouted the boy, as he ran away.

Sha'Tanya was relieved to be free, and amazed at how she had been saved from disaster twice, because of falling into a garbage skip.

"Lord, I owe You another one," she said, as she took flight again, headed for home, "I guess I can make it two days without insulting Emelia Harris."
Sha'Tanya mustered all of her energy and ran like her life depended on it. She wasn't looking for a place to shelter; after all that had happened, she just wanted to get home—preferably with all her hair gel intact.

Two minutes later, the rain stopped. Five minutes after that, Sha'Tanya reached her apartment block, thoroughly soaked. As she approached her unit, she had to thread very carefully to avoid being splashed by vehicles; there was an unusual number of cars coming through her street.

Finally, she reached her unit, and though she was relieved to arrive at home, she mounted the steps of her unit with a limp, defeated countenance. She had been through an apocalypse, just to keep her address secret.

"I hope we can get things back on track soon," she thought, as she gripped the doorknob, thinking of how her life had been derailed by the hurricane, "I can't go the rest of the school year like this."

In short order, she pulled the door to reveal a

dark, old woman with grey cornrowed hair, sitting in a chair.

"Oh lawd, my granddaughter soaking wet," cried the old lady, "get off those clothes as soon as possible!"

Just then, Sha'Tanya heard someone shout her name.

"Sha'Tanya?" came the voice.

Sha'Tanya spun around to see the most horrible sight imaginable—Lystra, in the front seat of her father's car, stopped right outside her house.

"A tree was in the road and we had to make a major detour and got lost," started Lystra, "been rambling about, following cars for a while now."

"Girl, listen to your grandmother," cried the old woman, appearing in the doorway, "come inside and take off those clothes—and bathe, 'cause you smell stink!"

"Grandmother?" cried Lystra. "Tan Tan, what the bird!"

In that moment, Laurel's words echoed in Sha'Tanya's head.

"Lystra is a good friend, but you know she's an unplugged fridge—can't keep anything for long!"

All Sha'Tanya could do was whisper another prayer.

"Lord, I know I asked for a lot today," she whispered, "but, please, keep this fridge plugged in."

LADY CARTER

Sha'Tanya stood in an off-white bathroom, over a sink, in front of a mirror, fixing her new, fourth-form school uniform and seeking to make herself as fresh as possible. A tall, bony, fair skinned girl with a shoulder length ponytail entered the bathroom, with a backpack in hand, and made her way over to the mirror, next to Sha'Tanya.

"You are next to me, Emelia Harris," said Sha'Tanya, coldly, as she stared at the girl's reflection in the mirror. "Error!"

"The real error," started Emelia, with a smirk, "is you, in front of this mirror, trying to succeed where creation failed."

Sha'Tanya turned her body to look directly at Emelia, with fire in her eyes.

"No hips, no bosom, fake ponytail and bony, hard feet like two tamarind rods …" she cried, cutting her eyes at Emelia, "if creation failed me, that means it ain't bother to even try with you."

Emelia stared at her coldly, with narrowed eyes. Suddenly, her eyes widened and she started to laugh heartily.

"The loose screws in your head finally dropping out?" Sha'Tanya retorted, giving her a deadpan stare with folded arms.

"Yesterday, I bumped into you in the canteen," said Emelia, with a smile.

"I remember," replied Sha'Tanya, with the same deadpan stare and folded arms, "I had to make sure I washed the area of contact properly."

"That ain't all you had to wash, sweetheart," said Emelia, with her smile becoming wider, "I put a pen mark on that skirt—and I can still see it today!"

Sha'Tanya stared intently at Emelia, with both fire and water in her eyes. A year ago, she had lost her house to a devastating hurricane, and was forced to share a cramped apartment unit with seven other family members. At that time, she had hoped this would be a temporary situation; one year and three additional housemates later, her living and financial situations were worse than ever, and she was very sensitive about both.

"I understand you' supposed to be going to watch the new *Celestial Soldiers* movie this Saturday," said Emelia, still giggling, "I' waiting to see what old, yesteryear clothes you wear."

Before Sha'Tanya could render a response, she heard a toilet flush in one of the stalls, deeper in the bathroom. A small ray of hope penetrated her dark countenance as a tall, thick, dark girl with corn rows exited one of the stalls and marched towards Emelia like a raging bull; it was her best friend, Laurel.

"I' going to hit you so hard, you' going to grow some hips," cried Laurel as she stomped towards her target.

Emelia's eyes widened at the sight of the hulking girl and evacuated the bathroom like a teargassed criminal.

With Emelia dispatched, Laurel proceeded to hug Sha'Tanya, who was trying to dry the tears from her eyes.

"Forget about that flat, bony yard fowl," said Laurel, tightening her embrace.

"That 'fowl-cock' knows I only have one uniform," said Sha'Tanya in a distressed tone.

In short order, the tears were dried and Laurel placed one arm around Sha'Tanya's shoulder and led her out of the bathroom.

"I managed to keep my address secret for a whole year," started Sha'Tanya, as she walked with Laurel back to their classroom, "and now, Emelia Harris, of all people, knows how poor my family is."

"Being poor ain't shameful; a lot of people live in poverty, including me," said Laurel, maintaining her one-arm embrace as they approached a flight of stairs leading to the classroom. "Face the reality and work on your grades so you can better yourself in the future."

"Error!" cried Sha'Tanya, breaking the embrace at the foot of the staircase. "I ain't going to be known as the dirt-poor girl from the ghetto; I' going to the theatre to watch the new 'flim' for *Celestial Soldiers* this weekend—and I will only be seen in the latest styles!"

"Girl, that ain't important," cried Laurel, holding her head, "focus on your grades; you barely made it into fourth form!"

"Be cool, I got this," replied Sha'Tanya, calmly, with her hands in a defensive posture. "Dashawn can get me some hot threads for a quarter of the price."

Laurel's face turned red as she folded her arms and stared at Sha'Tanya with narrowed eyes.

"You mean the same Dashawn from 'Dead Sea High' that tried to take advantage of you two years ago?" cried Laurel, angrily. "You mean to tell me you learned nothing?"

"Be cool; he can't take advantage of me in a packed theatre," Sha'Tanya replied, in an indifferent tone, "and I really need the clothes."

"Sha'Tanya, he is a womanizer, an abuser and a big, stinking thief!" cried Laurel, angrily as her huge hand lashed the metal staircase with force. "I would slap you so hard you would swear the hurricane came back!"

"Alright!" cried Sha'Tanya, startled as the metal railing continued to vibrate from Laurel's lash. "No more Dashawn; I'll find another way—somehow."

Laurel just grunted and proceeded to storm up the stairs to the classroom, as the vibrations started to subside.

Sha'Tanya stood at the bottom of the stairs for a moment, pondering.

"Laurel was right; the clothes ain't worth getting mixed up with Dashawn again," she thought, as the bell rang, signalling the end of recess. "I gotta cut him off this evening—but I ain't about to let poverty destroy my image. Error."

Suddenly, a brown, medium height, medium build girl with her hair gelled into a bun, ran up to her and pulled her aside; it was her friend, Lystra, the only other person who knew the truth about her living conditions.

"I was just outside the staffroom and overheard … there's a gas leak in the area—no more classes for the day," said Lystra, excitedly. "They're going to let the children call their parents to collect them, so you could start planning your afternoon off!"

"Boom!" cried Sha'Tanya, smiling widely as she nodded her head. "I just figured out how to update my wardrobe—free of danger, and free of cost."

Thirty minutes later, Sha'Tanya was in the school parking lot, watching a sleek, red coupé approach. The car caused quite a stir as children pointed and stared admiringly at its polished body. Sha'Tanya was admiring the car as well, but was apprehensive about what its arrival entailed.

Finally, the car came to a stop next to her, and the driver's window came down.

"Good afternoon, thanks for coming, Aunty Drucilla," said Sha'Tanya, to a dark, slender woman, in a yellow linen dress with a pearl necklace and an extravagant hairstyle supported by a myriad of concealed hairpins.

The woman gave Sha'Tanya an intent stare with wide eyes as she pushed her head backwards a bit.

"Thanks for coming, Lady Carter," Sha'Tanya corrected herself, promptly, "I didn't expect you to get here so quickly."

"Good evening. I was already on the road," started the woman, with a pleasant smile, "fortunately, you have an aunt who can be reached while mobile. Now come, get into the coupé."

"You mean the car?" asked Sha'Tanya, with a quizzical look.

"These things around us are cars," replied Lady Carter, sharply with wide eyes, as she gestured to the other vehicles in the parking lot. "This, my dear child, is a coupé—a prestigious vehicle with two doors and a sloping rear roofline."

"This woman thinks she's the greatest thing since the invention of hair gel," Sha'Tanya thought to herself, before subduing and veiling the thought in a highly deceitful pleasantry.

"Thank you for 'learning' me the difference," she said with a smile before walking around the car, pulling the door, descending into the black, leather seat and closing the door again.

"For the record," said Lady Carter, as she raised her window, adjusted the air conditioner and started to drive, "I did not 'learn' you the difference, I taught you the difference."

"I'll try to remember that in future," Sha'Tanya replied, with a smile of further deceit.

"She thinks she's so high above the rest of us riff-raff," Sha'Tanya thought to herself, before looking around to see the scores of children staring at her in the coupé. She caught a glimpse of Emelia Harris in the crowd, staring wide-eyed at her through the window, and any negative feelings she had about her aunt became less significant; it would be well worth the interaction with her condescending aunt to give Emelia a richer perception of her.

As the car made its way around the school compound, to the back gate, Lady Carter enquired about Sha'Tanya's wellbeing—in her own unique way.

"So, how bad is it?" asked Lady Carter, maintaining a stoic forward stare.

"How bad is what?" asked Sha'Tanya, side-looking her aunt sceptically.

"Your life, of course," replied Lady Carter, in a matter-of-fact way. "You now live even deeper in the ghetto, with a financially embarrassed parent, in tight quarters with riffraff; that can't be easy."

"This woman forgot that she grew up in the same riffraff, tight quarters?" Sha'Tanya thought, as she fought with every fibre of her being not to instinctively utter the word "error" in disgust. As offensive as she found her aunt's words, she knew she was fishing for something, and she couldn't risk alienating her aunt until she had caught it.

"Truthfully, it ain't easy," she replied, casting her rod into the condescending water, "I have one uniform, and nothing to wear out; it's only a matter of time before people notice."

"Oh, the shame," cried Lady Carter, biting the bait as she drove through the back gate of the school, "it pains me to see you punished for your family's deficiencies."

"Excuse you!" cried Sha'Tanya, with attitude, verbalising her true thoughts for the first time, and jeopardising her big catch.

"Don't get defensive, child, I'm on your side," started Lady Carter, calmly, affirming she was still on the hook. "Your relatives are seasoned in ghetto life but there's hope for you to be so much more; let's start by getting you some uniforms and a new outfit—right now."

"You would really do that for me?" asked Sha'Tanya, in a shy tone, reeling in the catch.

"I told you I'm on your side," Lady Carter replied, as she adjusted the car's course and indicated she was heading to a prestigious mall outside the city; the catch was secured.

Sha'Tanya was offended at Lady Carter's opinion of her mother and family, but she needed those uniforms and that new outfit to silence the likes of Emelia Harris, so she kept her thoughts to herself.

Thirty minutes later, they were halfway to the mall, driving through a residential area with big houses, when the car suddenly went dead and rolled to a halt.

"I, I, I don't understand how this is possible," Lady Carter stammered, after two failed attempts to restart the vehicle, "this coupé is constructed with the highest mechanical standards."

"Under the fancy name, it's still a car, and cars break down," Sha'Tanya replied, in a matter-of-fact way. "Pull the bonnet so we can take a look; I picked up some tricks from Uncle Jimmy."

"This is not a car; it is a coupé," screamed Lady

Carter, hitting the steering wheel and losing her composure for the first time, "and I will not be seen fiddling under the hood of an immobile vehicle!"

"You mean a broken-down vehicle?" asked Sha'Tanya, fighting the urge to roll her eyes.

"It is not broken-down," cried Lady Carter, passionately, "it is temporarily immobile."

Sha'Tanya just raised her hands as if in surrender.

"Now, let me call the mechanic on my personal mobile communications device," said Lady Carter, as she reached into the back seat for a big, red handbag.

"Huh," started Sha'Tanya, with consternation on her face, "you mean your mobile phone?"

"Child, the functionality of this device far exceeds that of a mere phone," replied Lady Carter, pulling a sophisticated-looking smartphone out of the bag. The device featured a nearly three-inch colour display, a full physical keyboard and decorative chrome trimming.

"This is state of the art technology," she continued, as she found the mechanic's number, pressed a button to initiate a call and activated the loud speaker.

Instead of hearing a ringing sound emanating from the phone, Sha'Tanya immediately heard a voice.

"I'm sorry, but you have insufficient funds for this call."

"I do not have insufficient funds," cried Lady Carter, sharply, pointing a finger at Sha'Tanya before she could say anything. "You depleted my credit when you called me from the school landline; I just have to buy a phone card."

"From where?" asked Sha'Tanya, looking around her at their present environment.

"As degrading as it is, I will take a walk until I find a phone booth," started Lady Carter, "there should be one in every area. You stay here and guard the coupé with your life."

"Guard? Cool," said Sha'Tanya, with a snarky attitude. "With my life? Error!"

"You know I have abolished the word 'error' in my presence," said Lady Carter, sternly, as she exited the vehicle with her handbag and Sha'Tanya rolled her eyes. "Now, come and help me."

Sha'Tanya exited the car with piqued curiosity and promptly joined her aunt at the front of the vehicle. She looked on with great consternation as Lady Carter retrieved a small screwdriver from her handbag, and started to unfasten the front license plate.

"What madness is this?" cried Sha'Tanya, as Lady Carter gave her the plate to hold.

"Madness?" cried Lady Carter, giving her an intent stare with wide eyes as she pushed her head backwards a bit. "You think I'm allowing anyone to recognise my coupé in this immobile state?"

"A breakdown ain't shameful; a lot of cars break down every day," cried Sha'Tanya, emphatically.

"Unacceptable," cried Lady Carter, with contempt in her voice, "a breakdown will never be the norm for me, and nobody will be allowed to form that opinion!"

Lady Carter proceeded to the rear of the vehicle and unscrewed the rear license plate as well, before instructing Sha'Tanya to assist her in stuffing them into her handbag. With the plates sequestered, Lady Carter set off on her journey to find a phone booth, with her red handbag, and red shoes with five-centimetre-tall wedge heels, leaving Sha'Tanya behind with the key.

One hour later, there was no sign of Lady Carter, and Sha'Tanya had descended into abject boredom. Apart from the occasional window-peeper, and the two cars which had passed within the hour, there was no activity whatsoever in the area.

"Something better happen soon," Sha'Tanya thought to herself, "before I end up in a coma."

Just then, as if in response to her thought, a big truck, labelled "Ministry of Transport", drove past the car, stopped, and reversed to park right in front of it.

As two men exited the truck, Sha'Tanya exited the car to see if she could elicit assistance from them. One of the men was dark, burly and bald with a bushy beard, moustache, sideburns and a potbelly. The other man was clear, slim, lanky and clean-shaven with short hair. Before Sha'Tanya could make any request, the burly man addressed her.

"How you got out here already when school ain't finished yet," started the man, in a voice rougher than coconut on a grater, "and why you in this abandoned vehicle?"

"Error," said Sha'Tanya, arms akimbo, "we got released early and this car ain't abandoned; my aunt just went to call the mechanic."

"Well, somebody reported an abandoned vehicle," said the clean-shaven man.

"You ever saw a car in use without plates, Randy?" asked the burly man, looking at the clean-shaven man.

"Never," came the reply, "get the hook."

"Error! You ain't serious right now!" cried Sha'Tanya, as the men proceeded to attach a tow hook to the car. She wanted to explain what had happened to the plates but she thought her aunt's actions were too ridiculous for anyone to believe.

"How could the car be abandoned when I have the key?" Sha'Tanya shouted, waving the key around frantically.

"This far from school, this early, with the key to a car without plates …" started Randy, with a quizzical look, "take my advice, Frank; get that key while I call the police."

"Error!" cried Sha'Tanya, as she took off down the street like a rocket, with Frank in hot pursuit.

"What the bird," Sha'Tanya thought as she ran, "my ign'rant aunt should be the one getting chased."

Fortunately for Sha'Tanya, the burly, potbelly man was unable to match her stamina. By the time she reached the end of the street, she glanced behind her to see the man on his knees, gasping for breath. Sha'Tanya disappeared around the corner at the end of the street as Randy shouted to Frank.

"Forget it, Frank," he cried, "we need to get back to the depot—and you need to get to a gym!"

By the time Sha'Tanya reappeared to assess the situation, the car was gone and the road was deserted. She made her way to the scene of the breakdown, leaned against a guard wall, and waited for her aunt to return with folded arms.

Her aunt did return, about fifteen minutes later, winded, sweat soaked and livid.

"Where is my coupé!" cried Lady Carter in a rage as she approached the scene.

Sha'Tanya calmly waited until she arrived before rendering a response.

"It seems somebody filed an abandoned vehicle report," started Sha'Tanya, still leaning against the guard wall, giving her aunt a deadpan stare, "and the transport ministry towed it—with my backpack inside!"

"Number one—how could somebody think my prestigious coupé was abandoned?" cried Lady Carter, holding her head. "Number two—how could you allow them to take my coupé?"

"Number one—somebody removed the registration plates," started Sha'Tanya, leaving the wall and sticking her chest out, arms akimbo, "and number two—somebody … removed … the registration plates!"

Sha'Tanya wasn't sure where she stood with her aunt after giving her such a spirited response. To her relief, Lady Carter discarded her angry demeanour, took a deep breath and then proceeded to place one arm around Sha'Tanya's shoulder; she was still in good standing.

"Sorry Sha'Tanya, I was so busy trying to avoid shame that I ended up putting us in an even more shameful position," she said, in a low, defeated tone. "Now I don't even know what to say to the mechanic when he gets here."

"Simple; ask the mechanic for a ride to the transport ministry," Sha'Tanya replied, capitalising on her good standing, "so we could get back the car and go for my clothes."

Fifteen minutes later, the mechanic arrived in a grey, dilapidated four-door sedan.

"We can't go to the ministry in that rust-bucket," Lady Carter whispered to Sha'Tanya as the vehicle stopped in front of them, on the other side of the road.

"Normally, I would agree," Sha'Tanya replied, pushing her aunt forward to the dilapidated vehicle, "but right now, we ain't got much of a choice."

The windshield was cracked, the paint was peeling, door handles were missing, the body was full of dents and there were rusting holes in the doors. The driver did not look much better than the vehicle. He was of clear complexion but his skin was darkened with dirt, similar to his light blue, shabby, tattered overalls, which were greatly soiled with motor oil and grease. To make matters worse, he was sweating profusely. Lady Carter had the task of explaining to him what had happened to the coupé and soliciting a ride to the transport ministry.

"Woman, you on drugs?" asked the mechanic, after hearing Lady Carter's tale.

Lady Carter gave him an intent stare with wide eyes as she pushed her head backwards a bit. Meanwhile, Sha'Tanya nodded at the man from behind her aunt.

"Nevermind," said the man, before anything else could be said, "get in the car before it gets any later."

Sha'Tanya and her aunt both got into the back seat of the car, after the mechanic opened the door from the inside; the outer handle had perished in some unknown tragedy. Sha'Tanya entered first, positioning herself on the left of the car, leaving a visibly hesitant Lady Carter to sit behind the driver. The fabric on the ceiling was sagging, there was no air conditioning and the seat up-holstery was covered in miscellaneous stains.

"I bet Lady Drucilla Carter's gonna be scarred for life after this," Sha'Tanya thought, as the car moved off with an engine sounding like a lawnmower.

Thirty minutes later, the car was waiting in traffic on a double lane street, at a set of traffic lights.

"Good heavens," cried Lady Carter, suddenly, look-ing at a green car in the adjacent lane, "that's my next-door neighbour; I can't be seen in this …"

She stopped her sentence suddenly as the driver turned around and stared at her intently. Her sentence stopped but her body did not follow; she proceeded to fidget restlessly in the seat, bouncing her gaze between the traffic light and the car next to her. The driver turned to face the front of the car, but continued to watch her in the rear-view mirror. Finally, she assumed a slouched posture and held up her handbag at the window, blocking her head from external view.

"Alright, that's enough of you," cried the driver, "get out of this car!"

"How am I supposed to get to the transport min-istry?" cried Lady Carter. "How am I to get my coupé returned and fixed?"

"Clearly your parents never 'learned' you not to bite the hand that's feeding you!" shouted the mechan-ic, in a rage.

"Nobody 'learned' me anything," cried Lady Cart-er, in a condescending tone, "they taught me!"

"Get out, now!" shouted the man, violently, resulting in a prompt evacuation for Sha'Tanya and her aunt.

Sha'Tanya now stood on the sidewalk, next to a walled commercial property, while Lady Carter stood between two lanes of cars, next to her neighbour's green hatchback. Sha'Tanya looked on in shock as Lady Carter pulled out her mobile phone, dialled a number and raised it to her head.

"Hello, is this the police?" she cried, in a loud voice. "Thank heavens; I've just escaped a kidnapper!"

At that moment, the traffic lights changed, and Lady Carter scampered across the road to join Sha'Tanya on the sidewalk before the surrounding cars could move.

"You called the police?" cried Sha'Tanya, in shock at her aunt's actions, as the traffic moved off.

"Of course not; I have to buy a phone card, remember?" Lady Carter replied, in a matter-of-fact way, as she returned her mobile phone to her bag. "I wasn't about to let my neighbour think I got into that rustbucket voluntarily."

Sha'Tanya placed her arms akimbo and stared intently at her aunt, with her chest pushed forward; she had reached her boiling point.

"I can't believe this," she cried, as cars continued to pass by, "we lost the only transportation we had—twice—because of your ign'rant pride, and still, you' trying to keep up appearances instead of fixing the issues at hand! Error!"

"Know your place, child," cried Lady Carter, in a rage. "I would flog you where you stand; nobody speaks to Lady Carter in that way and nobody says 'error' in Lady Carter's presence."

"Oh, come off it, Aunty Drucilla," cried Sha'Tanya, rolling her eyes, "calling yourself 'Lady' ain't gonna make you any more important than you actually are; you came out of the same riffraff ghetto as the rest of us!"

By this time, the traffic lights had changed again and traffic was once again coming to a halt. Lady Carter sprang upon Sha'Tanya and gripped her firmly by the lower arm.

"I will not accept rudeness from a minor," cried Lady Carter, with fire in her eyes. Sha'Tanya had never seen her aunt this angry and not wanting to push the boundaries of this anger, she promptly apologised.

Lady Carter informed a humbled Sha'Tanya that they would have to walk the rest of the way to the transport ministry, and they set off on foot, with only an hour remaining before the close of the depot.

"I worked hard to get out of that ghetto," Lady Carter said, passionately, as they walked along the busy road and Sha'Tanya listened in humility, "I will not be identified as a poor girl from the ghetto; I will only be seen in the best."

Sha'Tanya didn't offer a response, but as she listened to Lady Carter's latest statement, she remembered what she had said to Laurel earlier.

"I ain't going to be known as the dirt-poor girl from the ghetto; I' going to the theatre to watch the new 'flim' for '*Celestial Soldiers*' this weekend—and I will only be seen in the latest styles!"

For the first time, Sha'Tanya realised that in some ways, she was not that different from her aunt. While they were very different people, with very different outward expressions, their underlying motivations were rooted in pride.

That afternoon, her aunt had insisted on posh names for herself and her belongings, removed her registration plates and alienated a good Samaritan all in the name of maintaining a certain public image. She had jokingly indicated to the mechanic that her aunt was on drugs, but now, replaying her own recent actions, she wondered if she was on drugs as well. She had insisted on wearing the latest styles to the movie premiere, despite not having the means, in the name of maintaining a certain public image. She had gone as far as reacquainting herself with an abusive ex-boyfriend, in the name of maintaining a certain public image—a decision which could come back to bite her if she ever made it to the movie premiere. Despite knowing how ridiculous her aunt was, she had reached out to her anyway, in the name of maintaining a certain public image.

As she walked along the busy road, in her aunt's wake, she was certain that just as her aunt's prideful actions had resulted in nothing but shame, her attempts to maintain her image would likewise fail. There was no way her aunt was going to buy her new uniforms and outfits after her rude, antagonising outbursts. She could still hear Emelia Harris' laughter, tormenting her hours after, and she feared that this would be her reality at the movie premiere and for the rest of the school year.

Thirty minutes later, the pair reached a major road, which was familiar to Sha'Tanya. Sha'Tanya's feet hurt, and she was drenched in sweat. Lady Carter was drenched as well, with one shoulder weighed down by a big, red handbag. Additionally, she was actually barefoot, carrying her red, wedge-heeled shoes in one hand; after an hour-plus walk to and from the phone booth, a fifteen-minute wait for the mechanic on foot, and a thirty-minute walk from their point of eviction, her pride had been overcome by her hurting feet.

"I think we are finished," Lady Carter panted, sounding thoroughly exhausted, "this road will lead to the ministry depot but there's no way we can make it there before it closes."

"Error," cried Sha'Tanya, "I gotta get back my backpack for school tomorrow!"

"Child, do not test my patience; 'error' is a ghetto terminology."

"Wait a minute; we ain't finished," cried Sha'Tanya, suddenly and excitedly, ignoring her aunt's last comment. "I recognise this road; this is part of my school route," she cried, "we could get a bus from here to the depot—and I can hear one coming now!"

"You expect the owner of a coupé to be seen in public transport?" cried Lady Carter, with her face scornfully contorted.

"What's the alternative?" cried Sha'Tanya, making a querying gesture with her hands.

"Fine!" cried Lady Carter, with a pout, as a bus barrelled around a nearby corner and approached them with music blasting.

The bus was adorned with spoilers, decorative roof racks, side skirts and red decorative window tints. The edge of the front windscreen tint carried lettering, spelling out the words "Road Warrior". It was packed tight with school children from South Sea Secondary, colloquially known as "Dead Sea High". All the steps were filled with children but the first, and a short, dark conductor, with a gold tooth and three gold chains around his neck was leaning through the perpetually open door.

The driver skilfully manipulated the gears of the swiftly moving bus to bring it to a stop next to Sha'Tanya.

"Step up there, sweet girl," the conductor called to Sha'Tanya, while gesturing to Lady Carter not to approach.

"Give my aunt an ease, 'Gold Rush'," Sha'Tanya said to the conductor, calling him by name as she hopped onto the first step.

"Where am I supposed to go?" cried Lady Carter, as the conductor signalled her to come.

"I ain't looking for all the long talk?" cried the conductor, "put you' feet on this step or get to stepping!"

Lady Carter stepped onto the first step, the conductor hit the side of the bus and the driver moved off with Sha'Tanya and Lady Carter hanging through the door with the conductor, who was hanging behind them.

Sha'Tanya was right at home, hanging through the door with the cool wind relaxing her body, as the bus dramatically increased speed; she had an unhealthy obsession with reckless buses. Lady Carter, on the other hand, started screaming from the time the driver shift-ed to the third gear. By the time the driver shifted to the fourth gear, he started to rock the bus from side to side and Lady Carter's screams shifted into a new gear as well.

"Be cool, Aunty," Sha'Tanya shouted to her aunt as the bus leaned to the left, bringing their backs closer to the road, "just hold on tight and you'll be good!"

Sha'Tanya's advice had no impact on her aunt, especially as the children inside the bus began to chant.

"Shakes, shakes, shakes!" cried the children.

"Be cool!" cried Sha'Tanya, as the bus continued to "shake" and her aunt started her own chant.

"Error, error, error!" shouted Lady Carter, shocking Sha'Tanya by showing her ghetto roots for the first time ever. "Put me off this ign'rant death trap!"

Lady Carter's screams fell on deaf ears, as the conductor ignored her and the passengers were fixated on the recklessness with tunnel vision. Her turmoil would soon come to an end, fortunately, as Sha'Tanya saw the transport ministry's sign in the distance and indicated to the conductor that she wished to disembark.

"Bus stop!" shouted the conductor, as he hit the outer side of the bus with force.

The driver ceased his rocking and manipulated the gears once again, reducing his speed rapidly and bringing the bus to a halt at a bus stop just outside the transport ministry. Sha'Tanya disembarked, but not before Lady Carter, who promptly removed herself from the vehicle as soon as it came to a halt, and paid their fares.

"We made it in time!" cried Sha'Tanya, as the bus sped off and Lady Carter tried to calm herself.

After the wild ride, Lady Carter was somewhat dishevelled; the wind had dislodged almost all of her hairpins, completely destroying her hairstyle. She pulled her hair into a ponytail and secured it with one of the few remaining hairpins, then led Sha'Tanya inside the ministry building.

After paying a fee, she was reunited with her precious coupé, and Sha'Tanya was reunited with her backpack. After reaffixing the registration plates, Lady Carter solicited assistance from one of the ministry's employees, who was able to get the car running in short order, explaining that the issue resulted from substandard engineering on that model coupé.

Finally, over three hours after the fateful breakdown, Sha'Tanya was seated in the coupé next to her aunt, exiting the compound of the transport ministry. Sha'Tanya felt defeated. All she wanted was a new set of clothes to save her from humiliation but she had crossed her aunt and led her into a traumatic bus ride; her entire plan had unravelled. What started out as a clever plan, had turned into an epic miscalculation. Now, she just wanted to get home and get a good, long sleep before facing the music the following day; by then, Emelia Harris would have informed the entire year group that she only had one uniform.

"It's been a long, hard afternoon," started Lady Carter, sounding just as defeated as Sha'Tanya felt, "but let's go get you a new wardrobe."

"R, r, r, really?" Sha'Tanya stammered, in absolute

shock. "After all that happened?"

"Absolutely—your image must be kept intact," replied Lady Carter, calmly, "on one, very simple condition."

"What's that?"

"My image must be kept intact as well," cried her aunt, with passion, "nobody can ever know what happened today!"

THE GREAT UNDOING

The cool morning breeze blew falling leaves over the school wall and across a quiet, desolate road. Suddenly, the quiet and desolation of that road was disrupted by the growl of a heavy, diesel engine as a bus barrelled towards the school. The bus glistened brightly in the morning sun, adorned with spoilers and other accessories. The name *Turbulence* was etched into its blue, decorative window tint. The bus was brought to a quick halt by a combination of brakes and skilful manipulation of gears. As blasting music emanated from the bus, children disembarked in a disorderly fashion. They pushed and squeezed through the door as others exited through windows; they were all rushing to get into the school before the bell rang. The last student to exit the bus was Sha'Tanya Carter.

"See you this evening, 'Red Man'," she said to the conductor, as she stepped through the door.

As the bus moved off, she made her way into the school, with her excessively gelled hair glistening in the morning sunlight.

"Sha'Tanya Carter is on the scene," she thought, as she made her way past the office and approached a long, trellised walkway leading into the body of the school. She was in good spirits and excited for the day ahead, but she had no idea how quickly that would change.

As she exited the walkway under the trellis, two girls greeted her with solemn faces. Her best friend, Laurel, pulled her aside; she was a tall, thick, dark girl with corn rows. She was followed by a brown, medium height, medium build girl with her hair gelled into a bun; this was her friend, Lystra, and she had a very nervous look.

"She knows," cried Laurel, in a frenzy, "Emelia Harris knows everything!"

"Error!" cried Sha'Tanya, arms akimbo with wide eyes. "How?"

"You really have to ask?" Laurel replied, looking at Lystra with narrowed eyes. "I told you she's an un-plugged fridge—can't keep anything for long."

"Behave, Laurel," cried Lystra, with passion, "I kept the secret for two years; it ain't my fault Emelia was lurking 'round listening to conversations!"

Lystra and Laurel proceeded to explain how they had come to school early to study for their promotion exams, not knowing that Emelia had done the same. Sha'Tanya wasn't hearing anything they said, however, as she instantly descended into a daze of despair.

Suddenly, she was pulled out of her daze by a voice which was grating to her ears.

"Sha'Tanya Carter—queen of the ghetto!"

Sha'Tanya looked around to see a tall, bony, fair skinned girl with a shoulder length ponytail.

"Emelia Harris," replied Sha'Tanya, in an annoyed tone, "I ain't in the mood."

"Girl, I would hit you so hard your grandchildren would feel it in the future!" cried Laurel, stepping towards Emelia with folded fists.

"Do it," said Emelia, cutting her eyes with a smile, "if you want everybody in this school to know where and how Sha'Tanya Carter really lives."

The piercing sound of an electronic bell suddenly interrupted their discourse; it was time for assembly.

"I own you!" said Emelia forcefully, pointing at Sha'Tanya with a narrow stare. "You or any of your friends do anything I ain't like, and I will undo your precious image like a shoelace!"

"I'm so sorry, 'Tan Tan'!" cried Lystra, as Emelia walked away, beaming.

"Don't mind her," cried Laurel, "focus on passing your promotion exams and deal with her next term!"

"Girls, I just want to be by myself right now," Sha'Tanya said to her friends in a low tone, before walking away.

As the entire school was making their way to the hall, Sha'Tanya was going against the flow, making her way to a secluded area at the back of the school. There was a garbage skip, an emergency water tank, and a non-operational kiln with the school wall providing a backdrop.

She dropped her backpack on the concreted

ground, leaned against the wall of the kiln, bowed her head and drifted back into her daze of despair, allowing the magnitude of her situation to sink in.

Two years prior, she had lost her house to a devastating hurricane, and was forced to move into her grandmother's cramped government-owned apartment with many other displaced family members. It was a tight fit and a massive cultural adjustment to share such a space with seven other humans. That number eventually increased to ten, and then to thirteen. Her mother's financial situation never rebounded, and with her father in a similar position, it became a struggle to obtain some necessities like school uniforms and other clothing. She was very sensitive about her situation and had managed to keep these realities secret, but now, her nemesis was in possession of this image-destroying information.

As she pondered what her fate would be, she noticed a shadow come over her and popped her head up with anxiety. To her relief, it wasn't an authority figure, but a slim, dark, third-form boy named Adrian. Sha'Tanya had met him earlier that year when he had unexpectedly risen to popularity. She had been on a date with him, going to a *Celestial Soldiers* movie premiere, because of his popularity. While that date had turned out to be a disaster, and his popularity was short-lived, Sha'Tanya retained him, not as a close friend, but as a mild acquaintance.

"I saw you come behind here and you didn't look too good," said Adrian, softly. "What's the matter?"

"My school life," said Sha'Tanya, with a sigh.

"If it makes you feel any better," started Adrian, with his arms folded, "my school life is probably way worse than yours."

Sha'Tanya gave him a sceptical look, as she said, "Error."

"I'm serious," said Adrian, gesturing as if to convince her, "this girl in fourth form has been blackmailing me for the entire year, making me do things for her—including giving her money."

"I can't believe somebody actually has dirt on a quiet, nobody like you—no offense."

"None taken—but you shouldn't judge a book by its cover," Adrian replied with a deadpan stare. "I dropped out of the ceiling in front of her while she was on the toilet."

"Error," said Sha'Tanya, with a chuckle. "Why … how …?"

"I was making an escape from Principal Harding's office, and miscalculated my exit point; it's a long story," Adrian explained, with a pout. "I thought I had escaped but when I became popular, she recognised me; now this girl—Emelia Harris—owns me."

"Emelia Harris?" cried Sha'Tanya, stepping forward off the kiln wall and gripping Adrian by the shoulders. "That fake haired, bony yard fowl is blackmailing me, too!"

"This is great!" cried Adrian, pulling his chin with a ponderous look on his face.

"Your head screwed on backwards," asked Sha'Tanya, arms akimbo, "what part of this could be great?"

"It's great because now I have a partner in crime," said Adrian, with a sly grin, "now I should finally be able to take down Emelia Harris once and for all!"

"It's true; you can't judge a tub of gel by the label," said Sha'Tanya, smiling widely and extending her hand towards Adrian, "I never thought you could be so adventurous and cunning—but I love it!"

"You don't know the half," Adrian remarked, as he gripped her extended hand and shook it in ratification of their new partnership.

That day, and the ones that followed, when Sha'Tanya and Adrian weren't appeasing Emelia's whims, they met in secret to build a profile of Emelia. They needed to find some dirt on her, so they catalogued every piece of data they could gather. Laurel and Lystra were busy prepping for their ongoing promotion exams, but Sha'Tanya had no time for that, and no need for them; Adrian had proven to be quite intelligent and she had great faith in his ability to come up with a plan to undo Emelia.

Four days after forging their alliance, Sha'Tanya and Adrian came to school earlier than usual, and had a very important meeting by the kiln.

"I've got a plan," said Adrian, with a smile, "this is three days now that Emelia visited the guidance counsellor's office at lunch time; something has to be majorly wrong."

"I agree," said Sha'Tanya, with folded arms and a sceptical look, "but I ain't hear a plan yet."

"Well, if she's seeing the counsellor about something serious, the counsellor should have a file on her," started Adrian, with a sly grin. "You're going to break into Mrs. Gill's office and get a peek at that file."

"You going senile, boy?" cried Sha'Tanya, arms akimbo with her chest pushed forward.

"Trust me; I've pulled off a bigger operation than this," Adrian replied, making direct eye contact. "Let me coordinate the operation and we've got this in the bag."

Sha'Tanya was still a bit sceptical, but she knew that Emelia hated her and believed it was only a matter of time before she made good on her threat to release the damaging info. Sha'Tanya agreed to the plan, which Adrian thoroughly outlined, but they would still need some help.

A little later that morning, Sha'Tanya approached Laurel and Lystra, who were sitting on a bench, under a tree, studying for that day's exams. After exchanging pleasantries, she filled them in on the plan and asked for their help.

"Girl, I would slap you so hard it would take CPR to revive you!" cried Laurel, angrily. "I told you to focus on your exams and deal with any fallout next term!"

"It's the least we could do, Laurel," said Lystra, before Sha'Tanya could respond. "If I wasn't talking to you that morning, Sha'Tanya wouldn't be in this position now."

At that moment, the bell rang, signalling the time for assembly.

"Fine," cried Laurel, forcefully, as she put her book in her bag and rose from the bench, "but this is foolishness; you need to get your priorities straight!"

Sha'Tanya paused for a moment, as Laurel and Lystra made their way to the hall for assembly. She knew Laurel was right, and looking out for her best interest, but she couldn't allow Emelia to release her living conditions; she wasn't going to be identified as a dirt-poor girl from the ghetto.

Recess came and the plan was put into motion. Lystra ran down the walkway under the trellis and dashed to a door in the middle of the office block, which was at the end of the trellis. She knocked vigorously on the door until it opened to reveal a tall, dark lady with braided hair. Sha'Tanya and Adrian were mere metres away, watching from behind a hedge.

"Good heavens!" cried the woman. "What's the matter?"

"My friend, Laurel … panic attack … classroom," started Lystra, in a frenzy, tugging the woman's arm as she spoke, "please, we need you now, Mrs. Gill!"

"Okay, okay!" cried Mrs. Gill, as Lystra pulled her out of the office. She barely had time to pull the door shut, before Lystra tugged her towards the trellis.

"She's good," Adrian whispered to Sha'Tanya, as Lystra flew past their position with the counsellor, "let's hope Laurel is too."

In short order, Sha'Tanya exited her hiding place and ran to the door Mrs. Gill had just closed. Lystra had pulled her away so quickly, she didn't have time to lock it, allowing Sha'Tanya to quickly slip through it.

On the other side of the door, Sha'Tanya found herself in a very intimate office. There was a desk facing the door, next to the door was a couch, which faced the desk, and around the room were lush potted ferns. There was a small glass window in the door, which was tinted to allow a person inside the office to see out, while blocking a person outside the office from seeing in.

Sha'Tanya wasted no time in running to the desk. With a racing heart, she started to examine all the papers on the desk; she found nothing. There were six drawers in the desk, three on each side, and she accessed them as quickly as she possibly could, with her heartrate steadily increasing. From a standing position, she could see the trellised walkway through the window in the door, and she was sure to periodically fix her gaze there. Time was passing, her heart was thumping and she was finding nothing helpful.

"This ain't good," she thought, as she completed her search of the fifth drawer without finding any useful information, "Laurel ain't known for her acting ability; I need to find something fast."

She was about to pull the sixth drawer when she caught a glimpse of Mrs. Gill coming down the trellised walkway. She was sure her heart would fail, as she franticly looked around the room for a place to hide. The desk seemed to be the only fixture with enough space to accommodate her body, but it carried a high risk of detection.

"I knew Laurel wasn't a good enough actress to pull this off," she thought, as she heard the counsellor's footsteps approaching the door. "What to do, what to do?"

In short order, the door flew open and Mrs. Gill walked into the office, closing it behind her.

"Lord, give me strength to deal with these children," she said, as she made her way to the desk and sat behind it. Once there, she promptly kicked her shoes off, making an echoing noise as they hit the back of the desk.

"Now, where is my pen?" Mrs. Gill asked herself, aloud. "Maybe it fell and rolled under the desk again."

Mrs. Gill pushed her chair back, and looked under the desk.

"Bingo," she said, as she spotted the pen.

While her head was still down, there was a knock on the door.

"Come in!" said Mrs. Gill, in a loud voice, popping her head up.

The door opened and a girl entered the office.

"Welcome, Emelia," said Mrs. Gill, "have a seat on the couch."

The door was closed and Emelia took her seat on the comfy couch next to the door, facing Mrs. Gill.

Just thirty centimetres behind the couch, Sha'Tanya was lying on her side, with her back against the wall.

"Now this should be interesting," Sha'Tanya thought, with a smile, "I didn't find anything in writing but maybe I can get the dirt straight from the horse's mangy mouth."

"So, how are you feeling today?" asked the counsellor.

"Stressed," cried Emelia, "I hate this!"

"I take it there has been no improvement in your condition."

"No improvement," Emelia replied, sounding distressed, "it happened already for the day."

"What condition?" thought Sha'Tanya, with her interest highly piqued. "What already happened for the day?"

"I take it you have been able to hide it well."

"Of course," cried Emelia, "if anybody found out 'bout this, my life in this school would be finished; I couldn't come to school here after that!"

"What the bird," thought Sha'Tanya, "this thing is even bigger than I thought!"

"I hope this isn't affecting your school work," said the counsellor, sounding particularly concerned, "especially now that you are doing promotion exams."

"No, I can't afford to repeat a year," cried Emelia, "the longer I spend here, the more opportunity people have to find out about my condition!"

"It ain't gonna take a year for people to find out, sweetheart," Sha'Tanya thought, "I only need twenty-four hours; now, hurry up and spill the beans!"

"Well, it's good that your school work isn't suffering," replied the counsellor, in a calming tone. "I trust you have a strong support system at home—people you can share your feelings with."

"No," Emelia replied, with a sigh, "my parents are getting divorced and that's all anybody talks about at home."

"Hmm," Sha'Tanya thought.

"Hmm," Mrs. Gill replied, "tell me, did you get back any results from the doctor as yet?"

"Yes, but he ain't find anything wrong so far," Emelia replied, sounding particularly defeated.

"Sometimes, when children are put in stressful

situations, like a divorce, it can result in such a condition," replied Mrs. Gill. "If you are stressed about the possibility of other students finding out, that may also be worsening your incontinence."

"Incontinence?" thought Sha'Tanya. "What on earth is incontinence?"

"Interesting," said Emelia, sounding a bit more hopeful.

"Try not to be stressed about the students," said Mrs. Gill, in a slightly more assertive tone, "and we'll tailor these sessions from tomorrow to talk more about the divorce; maybe the key to dealing with your physical problem is to deal with the emotional ones."

"Thank you, Mrs. Gill."

"Come on," thought Sha'Tanya, "give me more to work with; I ain't good with these big words!"

"No problem," said the counsellor, "and remember, there are other people suffering from incontinence; you are not the only one who relies on a diaper."

"What … the … bird!" thought Sha'Tanya, with her jaw involuntarily dropped, as Emelia exited the office. "This girl insulting and blackmailing people, and wearing a diaper? Error!"

Adrian's operation may not have gone according to plan, but it still yielded the desired result; Sha'Tanya had everything she needed to undo Emelia Harris—if she could find a way to get out of the guidance counsellor's office.

Suddenly, there was another knock on the door.

"Come in!" Mrs. Gill said, in a loud voice.

The door opened and Sha'Tanya heard Adrian's voice.

"Good day, Mrs. Gill," started Adrian, "I need to ask your advice on something, but I'm still traumatised from that incident that happened in your office; would you mind if we talked out here, in front of the office?"

"Okay," said Mrs. Gill, as she rose from her seat, "I guess that's understandable under the circumstances."

Mrs. Gill proceeded to exit the office as Adrian stepped back, giving her space, and reason, to clear the doorway completely.

"How can I help you today?" asked the counsellor.

"I was serious when I told you that I didn't want to be popular any more—and I'm not," started Adrian, as Sha'Tanya exited her tight quarters behind the couch, "but I've been obsessed with popularity for so long, that I'm still struggling to figure out who I am now."

"You're going into a new form next term, with new classmates and a new uniform; it's the perfect time to create a new Adrian," replied Mrs. Gill, as Sha'Tanya carefully made her way through the door and created some distance between herself and the office. "You're an intelligent young man; focus on your intellect and see where that takes you."

By this time, Sha'Tanya had cleared the area and Adrian thanked the counsellor and left to rendezvous with her, Laurel and Lystra at a predetermined location—the kiln at the back of the school.

"Firstly, thanks for getting me out of that office, Adrian," started Sha'Tanya, at the rendezvous point, "I had no idea how I was gonna get out of there."

Adrian just took a dramatic bow.

"Secondly," she continued, giving Adrian an intent

stare, "what's this traumatising incident that happened in Mrs. Gill's office?"

"That's going to my grave with me," said Adrian, holding his hands up in a defensive posture, "get to Emelia Harris!"

"You ain't gonna believe this, but Emelia Harris is wearing a diaper," cried Sha'Tanya, to a chorus of gasps, "some condition called incontinence."

"What's that?" asked Laurel and Lystra simultaneously.

"Loss of bladder control," said Adrian, smugly, "basically, she's peeing herself."

Laurel and Lystra put their hands over their mouths in shock.

"Come to think of it," started Sha'Tanya, with a ponderous look, "she always takes a backpack into the bathroom with her."

Sha'Tanya paused, and looked at Adrian quizzically.

"Wait a minute," she said, "I thought you dropped in on her in a bathroom stall; you should've seen the diaper."

"I was petrified," cried Adrian, as Laurel and Lystra gasped, "I was trying to get out of there as fast as possible; all I saw was the look on her face."

"Mrs. Gill said it could be triggered by a divorce, so it could be a recent thing," said Sha'Tanya, with a quizzical look, before dropping her analysis altogether.

"Anyway—it doesn't matter how long it was happening," she cried, with attitude and a wide smile, "all that matters is that it's happening now, and Emelia Harris' days in this school just ran out!"

"Wait a minute, hold up," cried Adrian, "we have a stalemate; she has dirt on us, and we have dirt on her. Nobody has to leave the school."

"Error," cried Sha'Tanya, arms akimbo, "she might get over this incontinence thing, and I might lose my leverage; I gotta go in for the kill now!"

"If you release the dirt on Emelia," started Adrian, nervously, "what's to stop Emelia from releasing the dirt on us?"

"I got it straight from the yard-fowl's beak; if this gets out, she's done in this school—completely devastated," Sha'Tanya replied, passionately. "I don't think you all realise how big this thing is!"

"Believe me, I know how big this is," said Adrian, raising his hands in a defensive manner, "and that's why I can't be a part of this."

"Agreed; this ain't necessary—and it ain't right!" said Laurel, passionately. "This girl could be emotionally unstable and you could push her over the edge!"

"I gotta agree with Adrian and Laurel," added Lystra, in a pensive tone, "if you want to make a deal with Emelia, that's fine, but I can't get behind this deathblow."

Sha'Tanya could see the merit in what her friends and new accomplice were saying; she knew it wasn't necessary to strike the deathblow. However, after spending the last two years protecting her pride, she couldn't let it go now. Emelia may have been emotionally distressed over her parents' divorce and over her incontinence, but Sha'Tanya was emotionally distressed as well; the hurricane that had taken her house had long left the island, but it never left Sha'Tanya. Laurel had urged her multiple times that week to get her priorities straight, but in that moment, keeping her pride protected indefinitely was her priority; no one could ever find out how poor she really was.

"Fine, you don't have to get your hands dirty," she said to the group, passionately, with arms akimbo, "but I gotta do what needs to be done!"

She marched off into the body of the school, intent on executing the greatest undoing in the history of the school. She saw a group of girls from her year group playing netball on the hardcourt and charged towards them, as Laurel came running after her.

"Girl, I would lash you so hard you would wish for a diaper," cried Laurel, "you gotta be better than this!"

Sha'Tanya ignored Laurel and barrelled her way into the midst of the netballers.

"Girls, you want to witness the greatest humiliation in school history?" cried Sha'Tanya, immediately capturing the attention of the girls. "I got a bombshell to drop on Emelia Harris; this bomb is so big that the children at 'Dead Sea High' will hear it when it drops!"

"I want in on this action!" came a cry from the group of girls.

"She passed me going to the bathroom not too long ago," came another cry from the group.

"That's the perfect place to drop this bombshell!" cried Sha'Tanya, as Laurel looked on with horror etched upon her face. "Forward, girls!"

Sha'Tanya charged across the hardcourt in the direction of the bathroom, with a throng of girls behind her.

"Don't do this, Sha'Tanya!" Laurel shouted, as she followed with the crowd. Her shout was drowned, however, by the throng of girls, who started to chant as they marched.

"Bombshell, bombshell, bombshell," chanted the girls.

Finally, the throng descended upon the bathroom. Sha'Tanya led the way, charging into the off-white bathroom, past the sinks and into an inner area featuring six toilet stalls on the right and a changing bench on the left. They entered the stall area just as Emelia popped out of a stall, with her backpack in hand.

"What's going on?" cried Emelia, looking at the throng of girls with a puzzled look on her face.

"My grandmother always told me people that live in glass houses shouldn't play catch with big rocks," started Sha'Tanya, with her chest pushed forward and her arms akimbo. "I can't believe you walking 'bout this school insulting people, and all this time, you wearing a diaper!"

Emelia's jaw dropped as the assembled girls collectively gasped and started issuing a chorus of exclamations.

"What the bird!"

"Oh, shoot!"

"She can't be serious!"

Emelia started to stammer, "T, t, t, that ain't true; d, d, don't listen to her!"

"If it ain't true, explain why you would need your

backpack to use the bathroom," cried Sha'Tanya, energetically, "or better yet, open that bag!"

Emelia started fidgeting frantically, as if trying to figure out what to do. Finally, she gripped her backpack tightly and charged into the crowd. Unfortunately, she failed to penetrate the throng, as the girls pushed back, insisting to see the contents of the bag.

"No, no, no!" Emelia screamed, pitifully, as someone snatched the bag from her.

Sha'Tanya looked on as someone pulled a diaper from the bag and waved it in the air.

"It's true, it's true," came a shout out of the crowd, as Emelia collapsed into a weeping heap on the bathroom floor. The unbridled laughter that followed was only rivalled by the sorrowful weeping of Emelia Harris.

Sha'Tanya had accomplished the greatest undoing in the history of the school, but as she looked at Emelia, wailing on the floor, she didn't experience the feelings of pleasure and relief she had anticipated. She found herself tormented by Laurel's words echoing in her mind.

"This ain't necessary and it ain't right; this girl could be emotionally unstable and you could push her over the edge!"

Eventually, the laughter was halted by the piercing sound of an electronic bell, signalling the end of recess. The throng of girls exited the bathroom, leaving Emelia and her backpack on the floor, but carrying the extracted diaper with them. Despite the evacuation of the bathroom, Emelia did not rise, and her wailing did not stop.

THE GREAT UNDOING

Sha'Tanya promptly left the bathroom, convicted by the sound of Emelia's wailing, but distance from the scene of the crime did not calm her conscience.

Two weeks later, Sha'Tanya didn't feel any better about the great undoing. Emelia had been removed from the school on the day of the bombshell drop, and Sha'Tanya's living conditions remained a well-kept secret—but this victory came at a price. Laurel and Lystra weren't speaking to her and with all the energy put into keeping her poverty a secret, she knew that she had done poorly on her exams.

It was the last week of school, and she had been summoned to the principal's office. She sat in the cold office, sandwiched between a big trophy cabinet and the principal's huge desk. Behind the desk, sat a tall, clear, slender man, with a humongous Adam's apple and a hairline in greater retreat from his forehead than a criminal from a crime scene—Principal Harding.

"I wanted you to hear it from me," said the principal, in a firm voice, "before you saw it on your end-of-year report."

Sha'Tanya's heart raced as she anxiously awaited the next line.

"This is the worst your grades have ever been," continued the principal, "and unfortunately, you will have to repeat your fourth year."

Sha'Tanya's world went dark in that moment; she descended into total despair. Laurel's words echoed in her mind, tormenting her further.

"Don't mind her. Focus on passing your promotion exams. This is foolishness; you need to get your priorities straight!"

She had spent the entire year fighting to save herself from shame, but those very efforts had resulted in an even greater shame. She had ignored advice, logic and reason, to execute the greatest undoing in the history of the school, but had lost her friends and a year of her life; she was the one who had been undone.

Coming next in the *Sha'Tanya* Series

Sha'Tanya
UNDERRATED

See the synopsis on the next page

Sha'Tanya
UNDERRATED

After a series of major upheavals in her life, sixteen-year-old Barbadian school girl, Sha'Tanya Carter, is repeating her fourth form year, and trying to right the ship.

Adversity surrounds her on all sides—at home, at school and at large. As Sha'Tanya struggles to do her best, and finally attain her promotion to fifth form, she has to face many perilous obstacles. From antagonistic family members, to aggressive classmates, Sha'Tanya has her work cut out for her. She even has to deal with overzealous police officers and draconian overlords!

Can she keep her resolve and determination when everything around her points to failure?

What will it take for Sha'Tanya to succeed in the face of such adversity and non-existent support systems?

Find the answers to these questions as you follow the exciting, live-changing adventures of Sha'Tanya, underrated.

Sha'Tanya also appears in the *Adrian* Series

www.marioherbert.com